P9-CLQ-574

THE LITTLE GOAT

A Random House PICTUREBACK®

THE LITTLE GOAT

Story by **Judy Dunn**

Photographs by **Phoebe Dunn**

Random House 🏠 New York

Copyright © 1978 by Judy Dunn Spangenberg. Photographs copyright © 1978 by Phoebe Dunn. All rights reserved under International and Pan-American Copyright Conventions. Published in the United States by Random House, Inc., New York, and simultaneously in Canada by Random House of Canada Limited, Toronto.

Library of Congress Cataloging in Publication Data: Spangenberg, Judith Dunn. The little goat. SUMMARY: Andy receives a little goat as a birthday present. He names him Sam and they soon become best friends. [1. Goats—Fiction. 2. Pets—Fiction] I. Dunn, Phoebe. II. Title. PZ7.S7365Li 1978 [E] 77-91658 ISBN: 0-394-83871-8 (B.C.); 0-394-83872-6 (trade); 0-394-93872-0 (lib. bdg.).

Manufactured in the United States of America.   A B C D E F G H I J   1 2 3 4 5 6 7 8 9 0

On sunny summer afternoons, Andy went
over to Grandfather's farm. He often stood
on the fence to watch the goats grazing
in the fields. They seemed to have more fun than the other animals.

But one very special day Andy did not stop to watch the goats.
It was his birthday, and Grandfather had promised to give him
a goat of his own.

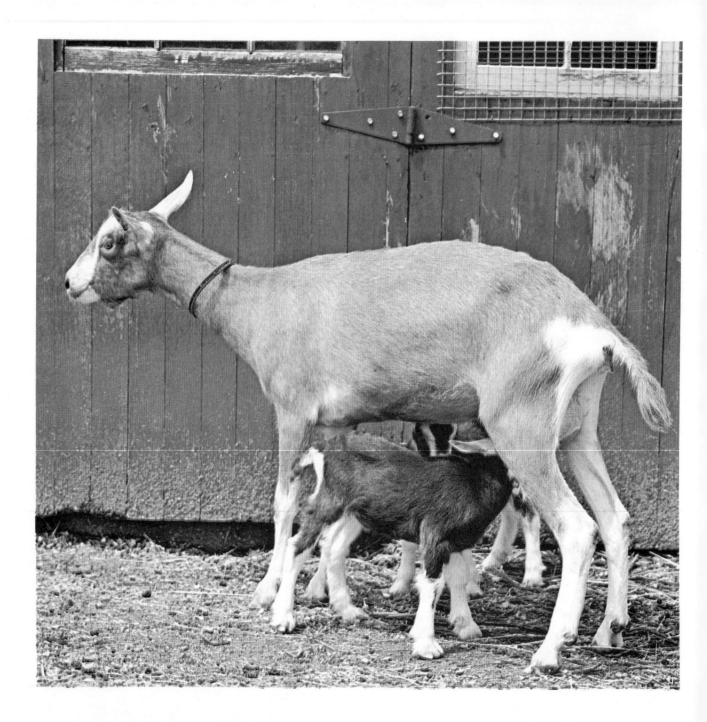

Andy went to the barnyard, wondering where his goat could be. He saw a mother goat nursing her newborn kids. Two frisky goats were butting each other playfully. And there were three busybody goats, poking their noses into the barn.

Andy had names for some
of the goats. There was Pops,
the billy goat who made
silly faces, and Grumpy,
the grandfather goat. Though
Grumpy's shaggy beard made
him look grouchy, he was
really very gentle.

Suddenly Andy heard a loud
m-a-a-a coming from the barn.
Peeking around a door was
a small brown goat wearing
a bright red ribbon.

"Happy birthday, Andy," said Grandfather as he came out of the barn with the goat. Andy hugged the little goat.

"I think I'll call him Sam," he said. But Sam was too busy nibbling Grandfather's hat to hear his new name.

Sam had a tremendous appetite. He always knelt down when Andy gave him his bottle. And he wagged his tail back and forth like a happy puppy. Little kids often get down on their knees when they drink their mother's rich, warm milk.

Andy and Grandfather built Sam
a special yard with an extra tall
fence. Inside the barn, they filled
his stall with clean straw.

In a few weeks the little goat
needed more than milk from
a bottle. Andy brought sweet grain
to his stall and Sam munched on
the hay in his hayrack.

As Sam grew older, he grew more playful. Goats like to climb and jump on things. Sam's favorite toy was an orange wheelbarrow. When Andy wasn't around to play, Sam would jump in and out of the wheelbarrow for hours.

One day Sam scrambled up the wall beside the barn. But climbing up is sometimes easier than getting down. Once he had reached the top, Sam did not know what to do.

"Ma-a-a, ma-a-a, ma-a-a!" he cried, until Andy came running to help him down.

Sometimes Andy spied on Sam
through a secret hole in the barn.
But one day Sam discovered the hole.
Like most goats, Sam was curious.

First he pushed his nose in.
Then he pushed his head through.
But when he tried to pull his
head back out, he couldn't do it.
Now Sam was stuck!

"Ma-a-a, ma-a-a, ma-a-a,"
he cried.

Once again Andy came to
rescue him. Andy helped Sam
get out of the hole. Then he
found his hammer and nails,
and a shingle to patch it up.

Sam nibbled at the shingle.
He nibbled one of the nails.
He tried to help, but he only
got in Andy's way.

Finally Andy covered
the hole so Sam could not get
stuck again.

Throughout the summer,
Sam and Andy played together.
Wherever Andy went, the little
goat trotted along, his tail
wagging back and forth. Andy
and Sam were best friends.

Soon the weather began to turn cool. Autumn came.
Each morning Andy brought Sam's breakfast in a bucket.
One morning Sam found out what fun a bucket could be!

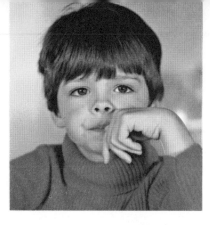

While Andy was in school, he often thought about Sam. He wondered what Sam was doing.

Sometimes Sam played in the wheelbarrow, or he climbed the fence to munch on maple leaves. But most of the time, Sam waited for Andy. When Andy came home in the afternoons, they took long walks in the meadow.

One Saturday Andy decided
to hitch Sam to his wagon.
Goats are strong, and can
be trained to pull small carts.

Andy fastened a harness
around Sam. Then he hitched it
to the wagon. Suddenly Sam
saw a bush that looked good
to eat.

Up the stairs he went.
BANG went the wagon, crashing
down behind him!

After a few days of practice, Sam was ready to pull the wagon. Andy held on to the reins and they trotted across the fields together.

On the last warm weekend of
the fall, Andy planned to go
camping with Sam. He put a pack
on Sam's back. He filled
his own pack with fruit and
granola bars in case they got
hungry during the night.

The only trouble was—Sam ate
most of the granola bars before
they reached their camp site.

It was almost dark when Andy finished setting up the tent. At first he felt a little frightened. But when he turned on the lantern, Sam snuggled up to him. Andy gave his little goat a big hug.

"Good night, Sam," he said. "I'm glad we're best friends."